1

8 Steps to Promotion

A Life Skills Guide for Teenage Youth
By: Nashauna Johnson-Lenoir

ISBN# 978-1-0878-6995-7

Index

Getting to Know Me   pg 6

Respect and Responsibility   pg 8

Respect Adults   pg 9

Responsibility   pg 9

Coping Skills   pg 10

Relation and Relationships   pg 11

Importance of Education   pg 12

Money Mangement   pg 13

Law and Legal Rights   pg 14

I am writing this book because I made a lot of mistakes in life. I don't want you to make those same mistakes and hinder yourself from being the best person you can be. Many adults growing up told me not to do this and not to do that and nobody wants to hear that, especially a teenager. They tried to warn me by telling me no but never explaining to me why without realizing that "no" made me more curious to find out why I couldn't do it. Adults sugar coat a lot of shit. I'm sure it's to protect your innocence but hey I'm here to give you the truth. Some will take heed (listen), some wont. And that's ok to. I didn't listen either as you can see but it was the tools that was embedded in me from my past mentors and their advice that later saved me from myself till' this day.

I dedicate this book to my first born, Iyanah. Happy Sweet 16th!!! Although I wasn't able to throw you a massive, stupid, dumb fantastic birthday party showered with a car and gifts like Tiana Taylor's; Instead I am writing this book as a guide of things not to do in hopes that you may be able to make our dreams come true for your daughter someday. In life you may not be able to do what you want, but to be blessed enough to do what you can is a gift in itself. Be grateful for the things that you can do, the things that you have and the important people you have in your life. They are all gifts. You and your siblings are a gift to me from God, and now I'm giving back. I hope it helps you some day.

Love Mom.

Getting to Know Me

Get to know YOU. The REAL you. If someone asked me to tell them something about Beyoncé, Jay-Z, the Obamas etc. . . . I could give you ten minutes of their business fast and easy. But when someone asked me to tell them something about myself I got stuck after telling them my name. In order for you to know what you want you have to know who you are. Ask yourself these questions

Who am I?

What do I want to be in life?

What are the things I like /dislike?

What makes me happy or sad?

By answering these questions about yourself you are indeed Getting to Know YOU. Write out 50 facts about yourself as fast as you can. This will also help you to get a better understanding of yourself. Anything in life that go against your natural way of thinking and feeling won't immediately work for you. Later on I'll tell you how to deal with that. Throughout life you may change your hair color, or may decide to be gothic today and a geek tomorrow. That's cool; whatever it is make the change because you want to, not because you see someone else doing it and you think its cool... It took me 30yrs to find out who I really was. Me myself I like my braids. They remind me of one of my favorite singers Brandy and my favorite movie Poetic Justice. But for some reason people like Cardi B and Nicki Minaj who rule the minds of majority young black girls, their style say that lace fronts are cool. I tried it and let's just say I'm still trying to grow my edges back. Everything isn't for everybody. If you try something, anything and it suncomfortable it's not for you.

I remember in 8th Grade this girl name China used to come to school with a pretty dress, purse and high heels every day. She was mixed half black half Indian. She was very popular, especially with the guys. I used to go home every day wishing I was her. One minute I hated her because I couldn't understand why she had the good stuff and I didn't and the next minute I wished to be her friend and hang out with the "rich" kids. One day I scraped my knee during gym and had to go to the nurse's office. I saw China there, she was crying. I gave her a tissue, she said thank you and started talking to me and would not stop. She went on and on about how her dad died and left her and her mom money and how her mom never has time for her anymore because of her new boyfriend. She had just found out she had herpes and was pregnant. I was shocked, this whole time I thought I wanted to live her life but at that moment I learned my lesson. Never judge a book by its cover. Long story short that same girl is now strung out on drugs and she looks very old and sick. Drugs will age you horribly.

At times middle school and high school can be rough trying to fit in with the cool kids. Everyone wants to wear designer clothes and shoes but reality is, that's their life. You don't know if that kid's mom had to go turn tricks just to buy those clothes. Or if that kids parent is a booster (thief). You never know. If the person that's caring for you could afford to buy you designer clothes and shoes I'm sure they would. Use that frustration of not having those things as fuel to help your imagination create ways for you to legally make some money. (Shoveling snow, racking leaves, helping older people, cleaning, selling lemonade, starting a babysitters club) something. There are so many ways to make money without going to work for someone else. You just have to use the gifts that you already possess (meaning whatever you are good at, do it to make money (legally). Until you begin to make the kind of money you want take the things you already have and make the best of it. Wash you gym shoes (including the shoe strings), iron your clothes and crease your shirts and make sure your hair is combed or bushed every day, make sure your teeth are brushed and has a nice smell. A neat, clean good smelling appearance is just as good as wearing designer rags. And don't forget to wear your smile with your chin up.

When you become an adult nobody cares what you wear. It's all about what kind of car you drive, how big is your house, are you married, how many degrees you have and what is your credit score. In the hood you're judged by whether or not you have decent furniture in your living room and how much food is in your fridge. The things you worry about the most right now won't matter in 10 yrs. Stay focused on the things that truly matter and that's your future. Create a goal, work your goal and stick with it no matter how hard it get (think of Rocky Balboa when he's running up those stairs in Philly) knock those goals out like its nothing then create new ones. PERIOD! This is your foundation, build on it. Keep building until you're drowning in your goals. And if along the way you so happen to forget who you are or what you want in life, do your 50 Facts to help find yourself again.

Respect & Responsibility

"Disrespect me, Ima disrespect you." That's how I looked at things growing up in school." Like why should I show you respect if you aint showing me any? Oh you wanna fight? We can do that to".

That mentality got me in a lot of unnecessary trouble. Look up the definition of RESPECT. Now ask yourself, what is your definition of respect? To me it simply means "Treat other people the way you want to be treated. "Not just some people Shauna, my mom would say. But everybody. Think about it, it don't make sense to disrespect your teacher, they have to pass you to the next grade. Why disrespect your parent? They are the ones who have to take care of you. Disrespect your peers, you don't want to develop a bad reputation, it's not worth it. Bad habits are hard to kick. If you make a habit of fighting and being disrespectful nobody wants you at their job, nobody will want to accept you into their college. Good girls don't want no rowdy boyfriend. They want someone who has money and potential. And guys don't want no hood rat, loud ghetto acting female as their girlfriend. What type of parent would this person be to their future child? Most boys would pass on a girl like that.

Ladies, respect yourself. If you don't want a man to treat you like a whore don't hang with girls with whorish behaviors. You know the ones that's giving out they body parts to any and everybody that'll pay them a little attention. Boys want nude pics, young men will ask you on a date and behave like a gentleman because he possess a strong foundation. Get you someone who is focused and can help you move forward not someone who will become baggage because you have your whole life ahead of you. Imaging trying to carry this persons baggage with you every day to school, while you're studying, when you are at work. By the time you get ready for college you won't go because you are too tired from carrying the baggage of some boy or girl who needed to seek help from social services or a psychiatrist a long time ago. You are not a Social worker or therapist stop trying to fix everybody's life. Stay focused on YOU. You still have a long way to go.

I'm not gone lie, I was the one hanging out with friends that had whorish behaviors. In 8th grade my friends went to parties, was drinking, getting high having sex all of the above and I figured hey that's their business I'm not doing that stuff so I'm not a hoe. Well one day we all went to a party and all my friends went downstairs to the basement with some guys and was giving it up and this one college student from out of town decided he wasn't taking no for an answer. After telling him no several times as he began to snatch off my pants and my braw he said "Don't try to act all innocent, you know you a bust down just like your friends." And just like that he had taken away something from me that I didn't value before ... my innocence.

I say all that to say this, be aware of the energy you attract. Dress and behave like a lady people will treat you like a lady. Behave and dress like a whore that's how people will treat you. It's your choice, only you can decide what type of person you will be. I just pray that you make the right decision.

Respect adults

I'll keep this one short and sweet. Adults act like they know everything, true. But most of the time they do. This may be hard for you to hear but listen. They've been where you are, listen to them. One day they won't be here to drop knowledge when you need it so take it while it's free. I learned to respect adults when I was a kid growing up. My grandma and aunties would smack the soul out of my body for everything. Listening to grown folks conversations, talking back, trying to get the last word in. All of these things and more got us a butt whipping. Respect adults because it's the right thing to do. You wouldn't want anybody disrespecting your mom or siblings so don't do it to anyone else. I never thought
I'd be saying this but I appreciate every whipping I got. It taught me the right way to be. Everybody didn't get the benefits of an ass whipping so if your parents are trying to correct your mistakes that's just another way of them saying "I Love You".

Responsibility

Since we are on the topic of parents, Parents have the responsibility of making sure you are trained and ready for life at age 18.It's their responsibility to make sure you know how to cook, clean, bath properly. It's their job to make sure that you are properly educated and respectful to yourself and to others. The minute you do any of these things wrong, the first person the world blames is your momma. If you now your mother or father or caregiver work hard to teach you and take care of you, don't embarrass them by allowing others to think that you are raised by bums. It's your parent's responsibility to teach you and it's your responsibility to learn. Back in the day I soaked in every piece of knowledge that was available to me because I didn't have a choice. It was either listen or get your ass beat. Youth today have the option not to listen due to laws that are in place. (I'm not even about to go there). I had an aunt that actually BEAT me and I had a different aunt that whipped my ass. It's a big difference. Be responsible and do your part at home, at school, on your teams and at work. Know what you are responsible for and master that. The more you do it the easier it will become. The rewards for a job well done is sweet but you gotta do the job first. Too many people in the world want something for nothing. That's not how it works. Everything has a price. The rewards for messing up are plenty, try it and see what happen. Lol nah for real stay out of trouble. One bad decision can change your life for the worst. I'm a living witness. Respect yourself, respect others and be responsible for the things you have control over. That's Law

Coping Skills

I developed different coping skills growing up in foster care every placement was different. One home may be Muslim, the other Catholic and my families church was Baptist. Some homes had strict rules, some didn't. Throughout the course of your life you will have to learn how to cope with different people, places and things. By cope I mean to adjust. Not to fit in but to learn your surroundings and figure out a way to adapt and align yourself with the current situation without judging it based on your past experiences. For example, I used to live in a foster home with an older lady who had a big beautiful mansion like house. No one lived there besides her and me. She had fine china everywhere in her living room. Expensive rugs lay over the marble floors and expensive paintings decorated the walls. I dusted the china and fireplace, vacuumed the rugs and polished the wood every day. Sometimes twice a day if I was on punishment. Keeping the house clean was my chore. I hated it in the beginning but after a few months it became my way of relaxation. Later on I was moved to a different foster home that was small like a show box. My new foster mother didn't have strict rules like the last one. Often her and her daughter would leave dishes in the sink and clothes on the bathroom floor. It gave me major anxiety. I remember getting on punishment after telling my foster mother that her daughter was messy. To them it wasn't messy. To me it was because of where I'd come from. Later I learned that I should be quiet about other people's affairs and mind my own business. My job was to keep my OWN things off of the floor. That's an example of how I had to learn to COPE.

You will move houses and your neighbors will be different. You'll change boyfriends and girlfriends and they too will be different. Every year your Math teacher will be different, every day of your life will be different. Evaluate the situation and figure out how to cope. Never compare your today to your yesterday because no matter your argument it will always be different. Only God has the right to judge, we was given many gift but the gift of judgement wasn't one of them. I'm not saying settle for ever situation, I'm saying be patient and mindful. See everything from all angles before assuming. If it's something beyond your control, figure out a way to cope.

Relation & Relationships

Relations is just a friendly word for saying sex. I started having sex when I was way too young to be having sex. At first I felt pressured by peers because everybody else was doing it. But then one day Jeremy stuck his tongue in my ear and my vagina started to tingle and I became so curious that I let him go to 3rd base. It hurt so bad and I viewed to never have sex again, The day I lost my virginity I was 13yrs old , I got 2 STD's and got pregnant. My social worker took me to abort the baby and afterwards we had a nice lil pep talk over lunch at Dave and Busters. I couldn't believe I waited 13 yrs. to have sex and this was he results. After that day I vowed to only use my vagina as a survival technique. I was lucky to not have caught AIDS or HIV. Gonorrhea and Chlamydia will have your penis/vagina on fire and smelling worse that a dead fish on skid row. Having an STD is no joke. If you're going to have sex, wrap it up. Unprotected sex will give you AIDS and all sort of STD's you can't pronounce. Unprotected sex can also lead to unwanted teen pregnancy. I had my first child at age 15, it was hard. I thank God I had a foster mom who was caring enough to help me raise her right. May she rest in Peace. Having a baby at age 15 changed my life. I dropped out of school and started working at McDonalds. My dreams of becoming an actress got put on hold. All of my friends was hanging out, going places and I couldn't because I didn't have a babysitter. I was stressed out. Waking up at 2, 3, and 4 o'clock in the morning to fix bottles and change stinky diapers wasn't fun at all. It was exhausting as hell. If I knew having unprotected sex would put me in this situation I would have made better decision. I love my daughter but I wish I would have finished school before having kids so that I would be able to provide for them a better life. Don't be like me, wrap it up. Value your life because AIDS is real and it can kill you. Teen pregnancy isn't cool. You have your whole life ahead of you. Make the right decisions or your bad decisions will make choices for you.

How do you identify if a relationship is good or bad for you? Well for one it won't feel right and 9 out of 10 it's unhealthy. This can be at home with your family, at school, at work... anywhere. If it don't feel right it aint right. My auntie had a male friend that used to come to the house to visit often. He would rub my leg and blow me kisses when my aunt wasn't looking. That shit is not ok. Tell somebody because I didn't. There is no telling how many other little girls he did that to and got away with it. I call perverted old men "little nasty man" lol. Because that's what they are. If you are in a situation where someone is taking advantage of you, leave and go tell somebody PLEASE. If you don't go and tell somebody and you continue to let it happen you will suffer and it will haunt you for the rest of your life. Never exchange sex for money. It's not safe and it will make you feel like a whore. No matter how many years go by and how many times you go to church, in the back of you're mind you will always be a closet whore. PERIOD! Don't do it lil sis. Money is temporary, how you view yourself and the way that others will view you when you die will last forever.

If you are being abused in any way leave and go tell somebody. Nobody deserves to be abused mentally, physically or sexually. Verbal abuse to me is worse than physical abuse. Words stick and often times play in your head like a song that's on repeat. Most of the time it's the people that are closest to you that say the most hurtful things that impact your feelings the most. If a person loves you, they won't hurt you. Leave, go tell somebody. It's ok to ask for help.

The Importance of Education

Education is important because without a degree you can't make no money, SIMPLE. If I knew this back in high school I would have showed up, I would have done the work I would have paid attention. You can't get a decent paying job without going to school first. I struggled for a long time trying to figure out how to publish this book as well as my autobiography due to my lack of education. Keep going, don't stop, get prepared. Stay in school.

I dropped out of school my freshman year after having a baby. I went back to school a few times and life's circumstances wouldn't allow me to say. I had to work. Going to college is a must these days. Everything that's anything has to be operated by some system that they are teaching in school. I tried going back to school a year ago and was the oldest person in my class. That was weird, I was embarrassed. Don't play in school. School is gonna make you some real money if your day dream don't work out.

Money Management

Save, save, save your money. All of it, don't spend it unless you have to. Recently the government got shut down and black folks was going crazy. Majority of us rely on government benefits for our basic needs Food stamps, section 8/ Low income housing and Social Security. If the government that away how will these families survive? You have to work and save for rainy days. I noticed that white people come to work and have salad, cheese and crackers for lunch all week to save money. Black folk have $100 they eating Chipotle all week long and then complain about not having gas money to get to work for the next week. We have to do better. Save your money. If you are not rich, stay out of the stores pretending like you are. White people have more than we do because they've mastered the art of not living above their means and they know how to save money. When other races spend money, it's an investment on something that's gonna make them some more money. All other races come together with their money to build for their future besides the black race. Black people only come together in mass numbers for 2 things, BBQ's and a Police Brutality Protest. I pray that the next generation can change this.

Credit- Research it, learn all you can about it. America is ran by credit. If you get a loan on something like a phone or a car or some money and you don't pay it back on time, your credit score I just as bad as your background check when you have a felony charge. If you have good credit the bank will give you a house, a car, free credit cards with expensive limits all because they see you know how to pay people back on time. If you know you are not good at keeping a job or keeping your word, don't get a loan. PERIOD! Your credit is important, don't play with that. The best advice I can give you on how to get rich is to not spend your money unless you have to. Save it, get with a buddy and start a business, a little hustle (legally) and save all of your profits. Good luck.

Law & Legal Rights

Many adults don't know their legal rights. Hell I didn't know my legal rights until I started writing this book. Google your rights as a citizen. Google your history as well, as far back as you can. The law is meant to serve and protect. Not all cops are good cops and not all cops are bad. Just in case you go to jail I think it's important that you know your rights as a citizen. Please google them.

Whatever you do don't get a felony charge it'll ruin your life. Most jobs won't hire you, nobody wants to rent you an apartment and you can't get college loans with a felony. Do you know you can get a felony charge just for fighting? It's called a Domestic. Obey the Law, jail isn't fun.

It's currently 5:46pm Saturday August 31, 2019. I'm sitting in my room at my desk at the Zumbro Valley Mental Health Crisis Center. I've been here for 5 days now and I miss my kids. I'm here because I had a severe anxiety attack and couldn't breathe for 2 days. This is the result of having too much stress in my life. My goal is to someday teach the 8 Step to Promotion Workshop as an after school program for teenage youth in hopes to coach and mentor then in a way that they make good choices. So many people have given up on our youth today. You guys are strong, smart, pretty/handsome and powerful. Your ideas and opinions are

way cooler than my generation. You deserve a chance to be heard. You are important and you deserve a chance PERIOD! This book is just a brief insight on the amazing topics I'd like to share with the world someday. I'm an adult and people are still telling me 'no" till this day. Don't ever let anybody tell you no to doing something that you know is right. I worked hard for an opportunity at my goals and then someone told me no. I didn't let that one no keep me from searching for 1 million yeses lol. I hope this message reaches you in time. I go home to my kids tomorrow and I will start a new day, a new chapter in my life where I won't give up on my goals because one person in a position of power told

me no. I will continue pushing forward like Rocky. Here at Zumbro Valley Health I learned that life isn't about finding yourself, it's about creating yourself. If I can push past my anxiety and depression while in a mental crisis facility you can accomplish any goal you set out to achieve. I believe in you, go out into the world and make us proud.

Your friend,
Nashauna

P.S. Start building your foundation on the next page

Who am I?

Let's hear it –

BGC Group and our Stomp Group at the Pace Back to School Rally in Rochester, MN 2011. Thank you all for believing in me.

Juke Fest Winter 2017

Jr Davis Ladyz at Summer Jam 2018

Davis Ladyz
Summer
Jam 2018
been with
me from the
start I love
my beauties

UCAN YLA Award recipients in Chicago 2016. I created this award when I was 11 yrs old. Dreams really do come true, no idea is to big. If you can see it you can achieve it. My most proudest accomplishment outside of my kids.

YLA Award recipents 2018

As the Teen Director of the Boys and Girls Club back in 2012 I dreamed of designing my own Life Skills Program for youth toprepare them for their future and on this day 6 yrs later I did just that in the same building I walked in a few years prior to work off a speeding ticket. Dreams do come true..

For bookings please email **journie_16@yahoo.com**.

Be sure to also visit the Journie website at
www.journieproject.weebly.com
for more information and to
donate to our program.

Made in the USA
Monee, IL
30 October 2024

68984409R00015